Contents

For James

This edition published by
GALLERY BOOKS
An imprint of W.H. Smith Publishers Inc.
112 Madison Avenue,
New York City 10016

Prepared by
The Hamlyn Publishing Group Limited
Bridge House, 69 London Road, Twickenham, Middlesex TW1 3SB
Copyright © The Hamlyn Publishing Group Limited 1987
ISBN 0-8317-8665-5
Printed in Hong Kong by Mandarin Offset

More Little Bear Tales

Written and illustrated by Gillian Chapman

GALLERY BOOKS
An Imprint of W. H. Smith Publishers Inc.
112 Madison Avenue
New York City 10016

Grandpa Comes to Stay

Mom was busy tidying up the spare bedroom, as Grandpa was coming to stay. Little Bear and Little Brother were watching out for him at the window. Little Bear was really excited and looking forward to his coming — he was planning what they were going to do together. When Grandpa came he did all the things with the young bears that Mom and Dad didn't always have time to do — they had great adventures!

Grandpa arrived, and the bears rushed to hug him. Grandpa always brought them a present each, and sure enough there were two little packages in his overcoat pockets!

Grandpa had brought them each a yo-yo! What fun!

After Grandpa had had something to eat and a chat with Mom, Little Bear asked,
"Grandpa, could you help us make our model boat?" The little bears hadn't been able to finish it and Grandpa was very good at fixing things. He helped them finish the boat, and it looked terrific — the sails and flags were in their right places, and all the fiddly bits of rigging were tied on neatly.

Then he tightened the wheels on Little Bear's scooter because they had become a bit wobbly, and he oiled Little Brother's stroller because that had become very squeaky.

While he had the tools out, he fixed Mom's hair drier, put the mirror back on the bathroom wall, and mended the fence in the back garden.

"Grandpa," asked Little Bear, "when you've finished, can we go to the park and try out our boat on the lake? We could take my scooter too."

"And my stroller," cried Little Brother, "to test it!"

So they set off to the park, Grandpa pushing Little Brother in his buggy holding the boat, and Little Bear on his scooter.

When they arrived, the bears wanted to go on every ride — the swings, the see-saws, the roundabout and the slide.

Poor Grandpa had to go up the slide with Little Brother as he was a little young to go on his own. Coming down, his cap blew off and he didn't want to go up again!

"Let's go over to the lake now," cried Little Bear, "and try out the boat."

They made their way over to the boating lake. Grandpa was afraid the little bears would get wet, so he launched the boat into the water himself.

It sailed really well — there was a slight breeze and the sails filled out bravely.

The bears were thrilled!

After a while, they began to wonder how the boat would return to the edge — they had forgotten to tie some string to it, to pull it in.

The boat was circling around right in the centre of the lake. Little Brother started to cry, "Oh no, our boat won't come back!" Grandpa tried to reach it with a tree branch but it was no good — he leaned over too far and . . . slipped!

The water wasn't very deep — but deep enough to soak his shoes and socks.

Poor Grandpa! He wasn't very happy.

11

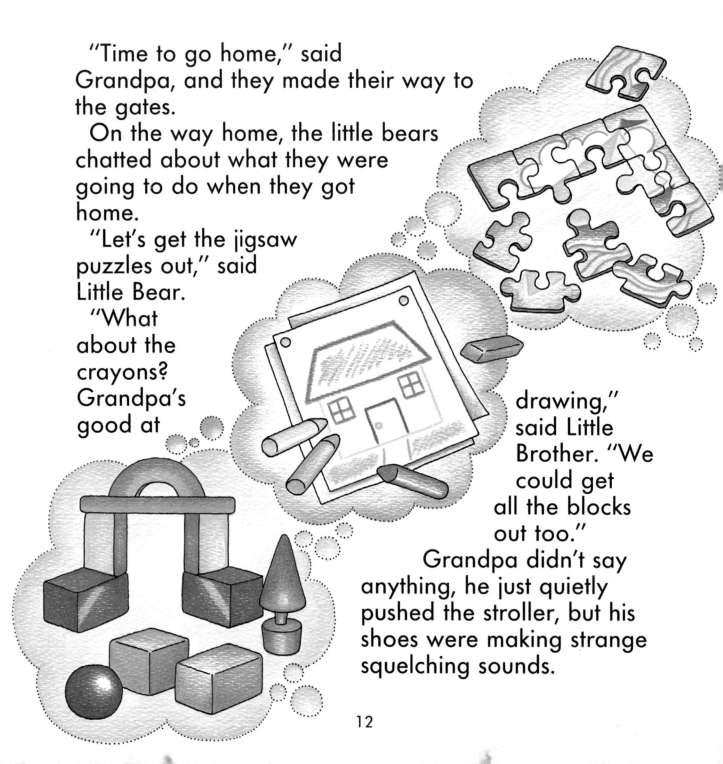

"Time to go home," said Grandpa, and they made their way to the gates.

On the way home, the little bears chatted about what they were going to do when they got home.

"Let's get the jigsaw puzzles out," said Little Bear.

"What about the crayons? Grandpa's good at drawing," said Little Brother. "We could get all the blocks out too."

Grandpa didn't say anything, he just quietly pushed the stroller, but his shoes were making strange squelching sounds.

12

Mom was very angry when they got home. "What have you been doing to Grandpa?" she exclaimed. His shoes and socks were wet through and his cap was filthy. "Off to bed! Grandpa's going to have a restful evening watching T.V.

"If you're not careful you'll wear him out before he goes home!"

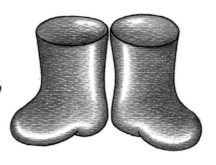

The Brand New Boots

The days were getting chilly because winter was coming. Mom was sorting out all Little Bear's winter clothes and putting his summer shorts and T-shirts away. He had some nice thick sweaters to wear and his green duffle coat still fit him, but his boots were too small for him now.

"Never mind," said Mom. "When we're out shopping

today we'll stop in the shoe store and get you a
brand new pair."

That afternoon they went to town and the first store
was the shoe store.

Little Bear tried on several pairs of boots and Mom
told him he could choose the color he wanted. His
old boots were red, so Little Bear decided on the
green pair to match his duffle coat.

He wanted to wear them to go home, but Mom told
him he must wait until the weather changed.

Later on that week, there was a very bad storm — it
rained very hard and there was thunder and lightning.
When it was all over, Little Bear asked Mom if he
could put on his brand new boots and go outside.
"All right," said Mom, "only wrap up warmly."
Little Bear hurriedly put on his boots — he couldn't
wait to try them out. At first, he just carefully kicked
some stones along — he didn't want to get his boots
too dirty on the first day of wearing them. He kicked

through a pile of fallen leaves and found an old can
— this was better for kicking — and noisier. Then he
found a puddle — well, he wanted to test his boots,
they might have a hole in them — so he jumped up and
down in the water, splashing everywhere. This was
great fun, and his feet were nice and dry in his brand
new boots! Little Bear was really enjoying himself now
— puddles were everywhere and he tried them all. Then
he saw a great muddy patch — he took a running jump

. . . lost his balance . . .
. . . with arms and legs waving frantically . . .
. . . he fell . . .
. . . flat on his face in the mud! Oh no!

Luckily, he hadn't hurt himself, but he was covered in mud. He slowly walked back to the house. He could feel the wet mud dripping down his neck, it was in his pockets and in his boots — his feet went "squilch, squelch" as he walked.   What would Mom say?

Mom was **very** cross!

"What have you been doing?" she shouted. "You only went out for ten minutes."

Little Bear kept quiet so Mom went on — "It's a bath for you, my boy, and straight to bed. Take off those muddy things now, and don't touch anything!"

Mom put Little Bear in the bath and gave him a vigorous scrubbing with the sponge. He even had mud stuck in his ears!

Little Bear had to go straight to bed even though it was early, and not yet his bedtime, but he didn't mind.

He really had had a good time, and he couldn't wait to put his brand new boots on again and have some more fun. He couldn't understand why Mom was so cross, because he *had* remembered to wipe his boots on the mat before he came in!

The Picnic

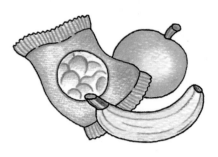

It was a lovely sunny day,
and Little Bear and his friends were going to have a
picnic at a nearby pond. Mom was helping them to
prepare the food—she was making the sandwiches,
while Little Bear packed crackers, fruit, buns, cakes,
cans of drink, and straws into the picnic basket.

"I hope you've got everything," Mom asked. "It is a
long way to walk home if you haven't!"

When the bears arrived at the pond they unrolled the blanket, and put it on the grass. Then they began to set out the food. It looked really mouthwatering, but the bears decided to wait before they ate their food and to play a game first.

They wanted to work up an appetite!

One of the bears unpacked the rackets and ball that they had brought along.

23

Little Bear's Little Brother was cross —
"There are four of us," he cried, "**but** only two
rackets. What shall we do?"
　　　Two of the bears start to squabble
over one of the rackets, and Little
Brother sat on the other one claiming
it for himself.
　　　　　"I'm having this racket!"
　　　　　he said.

"Come on, bears," cried Little Bear, "there's no need to fight over the rackets—I've got an idea!" and he went over to the hamper and got out two of the paper plates. "We can use these to ping-pong the ball backward and forward."

"Brilliant, Little Bear," cried the bears.

"What a good idea!"

The bears played hard and long, and they
got more and more adventurous with their
strokes, but all of a sudden one bear hit the ball
too hard and it landed in the pond!

The ball bobbed up and down on the water too far
out for the bears to reach it.

"What shall we do?" they exclaimed.

One bear suggested going home to fetch his fishing

net — but that would take far too long. Then Little Bear had another terrific idea. He sent Little Brother round to the far side of the pond, and gave each of his friends a drinking straw from the hamper.

"Now everyone . . ." Little Bear cried. "All together now . . . **blow**!"

All the bears puffed and blew through the straws and the little ball gradually floated over to the other side of the pond. Little Brother carefully reached out. "I've got it!" he shouted, and threw it up in the air. "Careful," the others yelled. "Don't get it in the water again!"

"I think we've had enough excitement," said Little Bear. "I'm feeling hungry. Let's eat our picnic now. Perhaps we could have another game afterwards."
Didn't the paper plates and drinking straws come in handy?